DEFECTIVE

D0016461

Aug 21

UNICORNS
OF THE
SECRET STABLE

Stolen Magic

JOLLY
FiSH
PRESS

Mendota Heights, Minnesota

By Whitney Sanderson

Illustrated by Jomike Tejido

Book design by Sarah Taplin
Illustrations by Jomike Tejido
Illustration on page 44 by North Star Editions

Published in the United States by Jolly Fish Press, an imprint of North Star Editions, Inc.

First Edition
Second Printing, 2020

This is a work of fiction. Names, characters, places, and incidents are either the product of the author's imagination or are used fictitiously, and any resemblance to actual persons living or dead, business establishments, events, or locales is entirely coincidental.

Library of Congress Cataloging-in-Publication Data (pending)
978-1-63163-400-0 (paperback)
978-1-63163-399-7 (hardcover)

Jolly Fish Press
North Star Editions, Inc.
2297 Waters Drive
Mendota Heights, MN 55120
www.jollyfishpress.com

Printed in the United States of America

TABLE OF CONTENTS

Welcome to Summerville
Home of Magic Moon Stable

Unicorn Guardians

A long time ago, unicorns and people lived together. When people started hunting the unicorns, two girls decided to help. They used unicorn magic to create a powerful spell. It closed off the Enchanted Realm from the rest of the world. Only the girls' keys could open the Magic Gate.

When the girls grew up, they gave the keys to their daughters. Since then, two young girls have always been the Unicorn Guardians.

CHAPTER 1

Bathtime

Iris poured soap onto her sponge. She lathered Rainbow Mist's coat. Soon, Rainbow Mist was covered in suds.

"I think she rolls in mud on purpose," said Iris, "just so she gets a bath."

"Watch out!" cried Ruby. "She's going to shake!"

Iris started to back away. It was too late. Rainbow Mist shook herself all over. Iris was totally soaked.

Iris laughed. "Okay, Rainbow Mist. Time to rinse off," she said. She led the unicorn to the edge of the lake.

Rainbow Mist walked right into the water. When it got deeper, she swam. Soap bubbles floated on the water.

When she lowered her horn toward the water, the bubbles turned rainbow colors and floated up into the sky. Soon, all the soap was washed from her coat.

The other unicorns saw Rainbow Mist swimming.

"Here they come!" said Ruby.

The unicorns thundered past. They ran straight into the lake.

Some unicorns swam. Some drank. Some splashed playfully. A few lay down and rolled in the shallow water.

"Bathtime for Rainbow Mist turned into bathtime for the whole herd," said Iris. She wished she and Ruby could swim too. The water was warm and a rainbow had formed in the sky. But it was nearly time for dinner.

The girls left the unicorns and went up the hill. They crossed the meadow filled with wildflowers. They passed through the Magic Gate and closed it behind them. Iris locked the gate with the key she wore around her neck.

From the outside, the Magic Gate looked like an ordinary gate. The meadow looked like an empty pasture.

Iris and Ruby ran across the lawn to the farmhouse. Inside, their mom was making a huge pan of lasagna. Aunt May was mixing salad in a big blue bowl. It was a lot of food for just the four of them.

"Hi, girls," said Aunt May. "How did your clothes get so wet?"

"Um, we got hot, so we ran through the sprinkler," Iris lied.

"You could have put on bathing suits first!" said their mom.

Iris shrugged and nodded. She wished she could tell the truth. But their mom and Aunt May had forgotten that they used to be Unicorn Guardians. Now it was Iris and Ruby's job to protect the unicorns—which meant keeping the unicorns a secret.

"Hurry up and get changed," said their mom. "We have a guest coming for dinner."

CHAPTER 2

An Old Friend

"Who's coming over?" asked Ruby. She snuck a carrot out of the salad bowl.

"Her name is Annie Octavia," said Aunt May. "We were best friends when we were your age. Then she moved away."

"She's back in town," their mom added. "We invited her to stay at our house for a few days."

Ruby and Iris went upstairs to put on dry clothes. The doorbell rang. When they came back downstairs, a dark-haired woman with glasses was sitting at the table.

"Annie, these are my daughters, Iris and Ruby," said their mom. "Annie is a scientist," she added.

Iris and Ruby smiled and said hello. Then they took their seats at the table. Aunt May set the lasagna on the table, and their mom set the salad beside it.

"Science is my favorite subject," said Iris. "What kind of scientist are you?"

"I'm an environmental scientist," said Annie. "Right now, I'm trying to clean up a polluted lake in Pine Cove."

"Lilac Lake?" their mom asked.

Annie nodded.

"You know that lake?" Ruby asked their mom.

"I do. It's a lake we used to swim in when we were kids," said their mom.

"I had no idea it was polluted now. I hope you can help, Annie."

Annie studied a bite of lasagna on her fork. She looked like she wasn't hungry anymore.

"I don't know," she said. "I have been trying for weeks. Nothing seems to be getting the water clean."

Annie set her fork down and then snapped her head up. "Tell me more about your new bakery, the Cupcake Castle," she said, a bright smile on her face.

Why did she change the subject? Iris wondered.

That night, Iris took off her key to the Enchanted Realm. She laid the necklace on her nightstand, like always. She stared at it as she lay in bed. The lake in the Enchanted Realm was clean and beautiful. She wished everyone had such a nice place to swim.

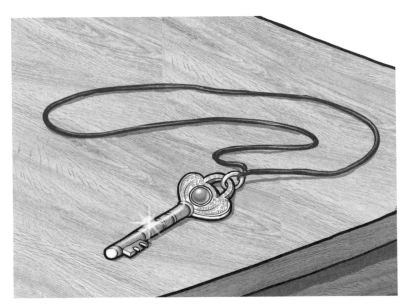

Iris saw the key on her nightstand when she woke up the next morning. But she decided not to wear it to school. She was always afraid of losing it.

After school, she and Ruby hurried off the bus together. Iris stopped to pick some lilacs near the house. She would put them in the guest room for Annie.

The girls went inside to drop off their backpacks. The house was quiet. Their mom and Aunt May were still at the Cupcake Castle. Annie wasn't in the house either.

"I'll meet you at the Magic Gate in five minutes," Iris said to Ruby. They usually visited the unicorns after school.

Iris ran upstairs. She wanted to grab the key she had left on the nightstand. But when she got to her door, she paused and frowned. The key was lying on her bed now. Who had moved it?

I must have put it there this morning and forgot, she thought.

Iris slipped the key around her neck. Then she went into the guest room to leave the flowers for Annie.

She noticed a journal lying open on top of Annie's suitcase. At first, she wasn't going to read it. It wasn't her business. But she glanced at it. When she did, she saw the word "unicorns." She couldn't help reading the rest of the page.

They grabbed their bikes and rode as fast as they could. They saw a sign for Lilac Lake. Another sign underneath it said, "CLOSED TO THE PUBLIC."

The girls skidded to a stop when they saw the lake. "It looks terrible!" said Iris. The water was brown. The ground was littered with trash. And it smelled awful.

Iris couldn't imagine giving a unicorn a bath in that lake. The unicorn would come out dirtier than before.

"There's Rainbow Mist!" said Ruby.

The girls quickly hid their bikes and started running.

Rainbow Mist was standing by the edge of the lake. Annie was beside her.

Annie heard the girls coming and turned to face them.

"What are you doing?" asked Iris. She was breathing hard after running.

"I had forgotten about the unicorns," said Annie. "Then I found my old journal.

I wasn't sure if what I had written was real. So I came to find out."

"You took my key and used it to open the Magic Gate," said Iris.

Annie nodded.

"Why did you bring Rainbow Mist here?" asked Ruby.

"A lake is an ecosystem," said Annie. "That means it is alive. It can get sick, like an animal or a person. I think Rainbow Mist can heal it."

Iris felt uncertain. Unicorns lived in the Enchanted Realm. They weren't supposed to leave it. The whole point of being a Guardian was to keep them safe.

Annie led Rainbow Mist a few steps to the water.

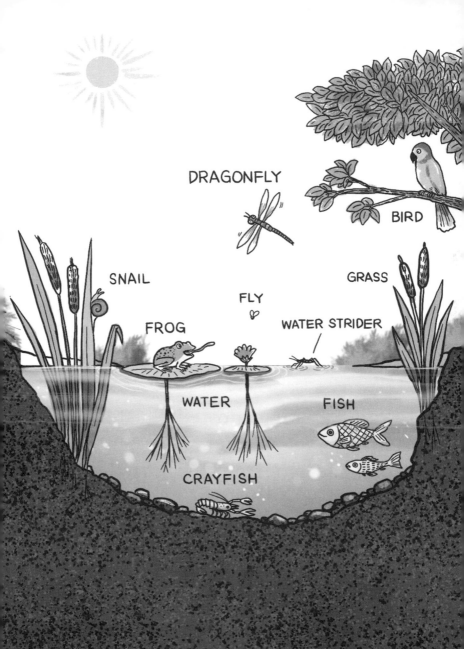

Rainbow Mist lowered her head. Her horn glowed. The water around her horn shimmered with rainbow colors. Then it turned clear.

"It's working!" said Ruby.

Rainbow Mist snorted. She fell to her knees. The light from her horn flickered.

"It's draining her magic," said Iris. "She can't fix the whole lake."

"I will bring more unicorns," said Annie. "You girls can help me."

Iris walked over to Rainbow Mist. She helped the unicorn up and gently stroked her neck.

"Unicorns belong in the Enchanted Realm," she said. "Out here, their magic fades. If they stay too long, they lose it forever."

Annie's eyes widened. "I didn't know that," she said. "But nothing I've tried has worked to clean the lake."

"Sometimes, I get stuck on my homework," said Iris. "I really want to look up the answers in the back of the book. But taking a shortcut never solves anything."

Annie looked out across the brown lake. She sighed. "Maybe you're right. My mind has gotten as cloudy as this water.

I wanted a quick fix. But this problem is complicated. It's going to take time. And maybe I can't do it all by myself."

"I'll help you, if I can," said Iris.

"Me too," said Ruby. "I would love to go swimming here someday!"

Annie reached out and patted Rainbow Mist. "I never should have taken her," she said. "The Enchanted Realm is her habitat—just like this lake used to be a habitat for many animals."

Iris and Ruby slowly led Rainbow Mist home. The unicorn's head hung low.

I hope it's not too late for Rainbow Mist, thought Iris.

When they got back to Magic Moon Stable, Ruby ran ahead. She opened the Magic Gate. Rainbow Mist walked through it. Iris let her go free.

Rainbow Mist crossed the meadow. She went down the hill to the lake. She drank the pure water.

Then she lifted her head. She sent up a shower of rainbow sparks from her horn.

Iris breathed a sigh of relief. Rainbow Mist's magic was safe. There was just one more thing Iris had to do.

CHAPTER 4

Flowers for Annie

Iris went to her room. She found the *Book of Unicorns*. The book had been written by past Guardians. It was full of information about the Enchanted Realm.

One chapter had pictures of flowers

that grew in the Fairy Forest. Iris turned

to a page that said,

The Flower of Forgetting

Makes those who smell it lose all memories of magic.

That night, Iris left another bouquet in Annie's room. Ruby tore a single page out of Annie's diary.

The next morning, they all had breakfast together. It was Annie's last day at their house.

"I'm saving half of my muffin for Rainbow Mist," Iris said with a wink.

"Good idea," said Ruby. "Unicorns love blueberries."

Annie smiled. "Didn't we used to play a game about unicorns when we were kids?" she asked their mom and Aunt May.

"Yes," said their mom. "It was so much fun."

"If only it were real!" said Aunt May.

Later that summer . . .

Ruby ran into the house. She jumped onto the couch where Iris was reading. She waved an envelope in the air.

"It's a letter from Annie," she said.

Dear Iris and Ruby,

Thank you again for coming to Volunteer Day at Lilac Lake. It looks much better with the trash cleaned up. I didn't realize how many people cared about Lilac Lake. I hope they will get to enjoy it for a long time to come.

I finally figured out a way to clean the water. I'm using aquatic plants. They will slowly filter out the pollution. The animals that lived here will come back. By next summer, you might be able to swim in it!

Your friend,

Annie

P.S. I saw a rainbow over the lake today. I'm not sure why, but it made me think of you.

THINK ABOUT IT

 Tell a friend about a time you had a problem that was tricky to solve. What happened that helped you get unstuck?

 Lilac Lake is dirty and polluted. Make a list of things you can do to help clean up your town.

 What do you like to do when you go to a lake?

ABOUT THE AUTHOR

Whitney Sanderson grew up riding horses as a member of a 4-H club and competing in local jumping and dressage shows. She has written several books in the Horse Diaries chapter book series. She is also the author of *Horse Rescue: Treasure,* based on her time volunteering at an equine rescue farm. She lives in Massachusetts.

ABOUT THE ILLUSTRATOR

Jomike Tejido is an author and illustrator of the picture book *There Was an Old Woman Who Lived in a Book.* He also illustrated the Pet Charms and My Magical Friends leveled reader series. He has fond memories of horseback riding as a kid and has always loved drawing magical creatures. Jomike lives in Manila with his wife, two daughters, and a chow chow named Oso.

RETURN TO MAGIC MOON STABLE

Book 1

Book 2

Book 3

Book 4

AVAILABLE NOW